The Big Bad Bully Bear

A Random House PICTUREBACK®

The Big Bad Bully Bear

Story and pictures by Ginnie Hofmann

Random House 🏠 New York

Copyright © 1996 by Ginnie Hofmann. All rights reserved under International and
Pan-American Copyright Conventions. Published in the United States by Random House, Inc.,
New York, and simultaneously in Canada by Random House of Canada Limited, Toronto.
http://www.randomhouse.com/
Library of Congress Cataloging-in-Publication Data: Hofmann, Ginnie. The big bad bully bear /
story and pictures by Ginnie Hofmann.   p.   cm. — (A Random House pictureback)
SUMMARY: When all the neighborhood teddy bears join together against him, Bully Bear realizes
that he would rather have friends than be a bully.
ISBN 0-679-87882-3 [1. Teddy bears—Fiction. 2. Bullies—Fiction. 3. Toys—Fiction.] I. Title.
PZ7.H6795Bi 1996 [E]—dc20 95-25976
Printed in the United States of America 10 9 8 7 6 5 4 3 2

Andy and his friend Sam were going to the park to play ball.
He put their teddy bears, Arthur and Emmy, into his red wagon.
"You bears stay right here in the wagon," he said.

As soon as Andy and Sam left, Arthur said, "Come on, Emmy! Let's play!"

Arthur and Emmy ran to the tire swing.
"Whee!" cried Emmy. "This is fun!"

"I love the slide!" cried Arthur.

"This is the best sandcastle we've ever made," said Emmy.

Arthur was giving Emmy a ride in the wagon when
he suddenly stopped.

"Look, Emmy," he whispered, "there's a big bear in our yard!"

The big bear walked up to Arthur and said, "Look at me!
I am Bully Bear, the biggest, meanest teddy bear in the world."

"I push myself to the front of the line!"

"I kick sandcastles down!"

"I throw little bears' hats high in the tree!"

"And now I want that red wagon!"

"Ha-ha!" Bully Bear laughed. "This is *my* wagon now!"

"He's taking Andy's wagon!" cried Arthur. "How can we get it back?"

"I could spread banana peels," said Emmy. "Then Bully Bear would slip and fall down!"

"Or I could bring my stuffed dinosaur and scare him away," said Arthur.

"I know how to get rid of Bully Bear," said Emmy. "Let's get the garden hose!"

"Gee! This hose is really heavy!" said Arthur.
"And it's all tangled up," said Emmy.

Arthur said, "Let's call all the teddy bears in the neighborhood to help!"

Arthur and Emmy ran to the corner. "CALLING ALL BEARS!" shouted Arthur. "There's a big bad bully bear in our yard! We need help!"

One by one, the bears ran into the yard and picked up
the heavy hose.

Arthur pointed the hose at Bully Bear.

"You can't scare me!" growled the big bear. "I am Bully Bear, the biggest, meanest teddy bear in the world, and this is *my* red wagon!"

"No it isn't!" cried Arthur, and he sprayed Bully Bear
with the garden hose.

Bully Bear fell down in a big puddle of water!

Bully Bear tried to get up, but his wet fur was too heavy.
He shivered and thought, "I need somebody to help me up."

"Help me up!" cried Bully Bear. "No!" the bears shouted. "You took Andy's wagon!"

"Please help me up!" he asked more politely. But the bears just walked away.

Bully Bear watched them playing. He felt sad and all alone. "If only I had some friends," he thought.

"I wonder why they won't help me?" he said to himself.

Arthur came up to him. "If you weren't so mean, Bully Bear, we would help you."

"Okay, Arthur, pull me up and I'll be the biggest, nicest teddy bear in the world!" cried Bully Bear.

Arthur asked, "How can we be sure?"

"Just give me a chance!" cried Bully Bear.

Arthur and Emmy pulled Bully Bear up and dried him off.

"Oh, boy! I really *do* have friends," Bully Bear said. "Thank you, Arthur! Thank you, Emmy!"

"I'd like to have a party for my new friends," said Bully Bear.

"What kind of party?" asked Emmy.

"A teddy bear party with lots of ice cream and cake!"

All the teddy bears came to Bully Bear's party.

Arthur raised his spoon and said, "Hooray for Bully Bear!
You are a real teddy bear now!"

"Hooray for Bully Bear!" cried all the teddy bears. Bully Bear
felt very happy.

After the party, Arthur and Emmy and Bully Bear waved good-bye to the neighborhood bears.

"Here come Andy and Sam!" cried Arthur. "We'd better get back in the wagon!"

Andy was very surprised when he saw Bully Bear.
"Who is that great big bear in the wagon?" he asked.
Arthur and Emmy and Bully Bear just smiled.

Who's glad he's not a big bad bear now? Bully Bear is!